A Note to Parents

READERS is a compelling program for beginning readers, designed in conjunction with leading literacy experts, including Dr. Linda Gambrell, Emerita Distinguished Professor of Education at Clemson University.

The ReaderActives line provides action-oriented images, colorful page designs, and stories in which children get to make their own choices. Multiple story paths encourage children to reread their adventures to explore every possible ending. Each ReaderActive is guaranteed to capture a child's interest while developing his or her reading skills, general knowledge, and love of reading.

Unlike traditional READERS, ReaderActives are not assigned a specific reading level. Generally, ReaderActives are best suited to Levels 2 and 3 in the list below. Younger children will surely enjoy making the story's choices while adults read aloud to them. Likewise, older children will appreciate picking their own path and trying new options with each reading.

Pre-level 1: Learning to read

Level 1: Beginning to read

Level 2: Beginning to read alone

Level 3: Reading alone

Level 4: Proficient readers

The "normal" age at which a child begins to read can be anywhere from three to eight years old. Adult participation through the lower levels is very helpful for providing encouragement, discussing storylines, and sounding out unfamiliar words. No matter which ReaderActive title you select, you can be sure that you are helping your child learn to read interactively!

Prima Games Staff

VP
Mike Degler

Licensing
Paul Giacomotto

Marketing Manager
Jeff Barton

Digital Publisher
Julie Asbury

Credits

Publishing Manager
Tim Cox

Creative Services
Wil Cruz

Production
Beth Guzman

The Prima Games logo and Primagames.com are registered trademarks of Penguin Random House LLC, registered in the United States. Prima Games is an imprint of DK, a division of Penguin Random House LLC, New York.

DK/Prima Games, a division of Penguin Random House LLC
6081 East 82nd Street, Suite #400
Indianapolis, IN 46250

ISBN: 978-0-7440-1947-6 (Paperback)

ISBN: 978-0-7440-1951-3 (Hardback)

Printing Code: The rightmost double-digit number is the year of the book's printing; the rightmost single-digit number is the number of the book's printing. For example, 18-1 shows that the first printing of the book occurred in 2018.

21 20 19 18   4 3 2 1

01-311220-Nov/2018

Printed and bound by Lake Book.

Making Your Z-Move

Written by Simcha Whitehill

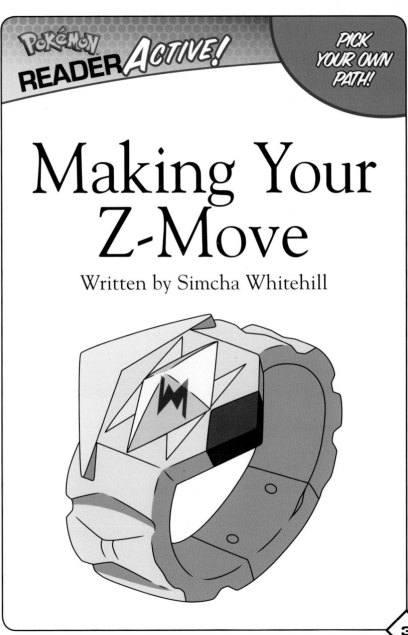

HOW TO USE THIS READERACTIVE

Welcome to this Pokémon ReaderActive, where *you* decide how the story unfolds! As you read, you'll find instructions near the bottom of some pages of the story. These instructions fall into a couple of categories:

1. Some instructions tell you to skip to a certain page–they look like this:

> Continue to **PAGE 31** and choose your first Pokémon!

When you see an instruction like this, simply turn to the page that's listed and continue reading.

2. Other instructions let you make a choice. This is how you decide where the story takes you! Each of your options is described in its own bar, like this:

> If you want Oshawott to make a big blast and ride the wave out, go to **PAGE 10**.

> If you want Oshawott to fill the hole gently like a pool and swim its way out, go to **PAGE 42**.

Whichever option you choose, just skip to the listed page and continue reading. In the example above, let's say you decide to choose the first option. In this case, just turn to **PAGE 10**

That's all there is to it! Don't forget–when you finish one story, you can start over, make different *choices*, and create a whole new adventure! Now it's time to make your first Z-Move!

MAKING YOUR Z-MOVE

Whiiiisssssh, waasssssssh. Whiiiiiisssssh, waaaasssssssh. The ocean waves crash then crawl up to your toes. The sparkling seawater is warm and almost as blue as the sky. The beaches of Alola are beautiful and you could spend every day here, but you have a dream stronger than the ocean current and it is pulling you towards your destiny. As a Pokémon Trainer, you have come to Alola to make your mark with your first Z-Move!

So, first thing tomorrow, you will start your journey through this incredible, tropical island. But there is still one question left to answer before you hit the dusty road: Which Pokémon will you choose to be your partner?

POPPLIO: Sea Lion Pokémon

HEIGHT	1'04"
WEIGHT	16.5 LBS
TYPE	WATER

If you want Popplio to be your partner, head to PAGE 6!

LITTEN: Fire Cat Pokémon

HEIGHT	1'04"
WEIGHT	9.5 LBS
TYPE	FIRE

If you want to travel with Litten, turn to PAGE 31!

ROWLET: Grass Quill Pokémon

HEIGHT	1'00"
WEIGHT	3.3 LBS
TYPE	GRASS-FLYING

To travel with Rowlet, go to page (39)!

"Pop pop!" Popplio cheers.

Popplio can't wait to use a Z-Move, too! You're ready to start training together because you know the most important part of Z-Moves is a deep bond with your Pokémon pal.

You and your pal, Popplio, head down a dirt path to the beach looking for the perfect place to practice. After a long stroll, you find a beautiful rock formation that juts out into the water. This should provide some space and it's far enough away that you won't disturb any of the sunbathers and Pokémon playing on the shore.

"Okay Popplio, let's start out with some stretches," you say. "Follow me."

"Pop!" it replies.

You stretch to the left. You stretch to the right. You reach down to touch your toes. When you stand back up, you spot a pack of wild Yungoos and Gumshoos heading up the path.

"I wonder where they're going?" you wonder.

To follow them down the path, turn to **PAGE 16**.
To stay at the field, go to **PAGE 7**.

"Popplio, I have an idea!" you say. "Why don't we see if you can make a bubble so big, I could fit in it!"

"Pop!" it says, excited for a challenge.

Popplio stands tall and points its nose up into the air. It then begins to blow a bubble. It starts out small like Popplio's pink nose. Then it becomes as big as a Berry. It soon becomes as big as your head!

"Wow!" an impressed stranger shouts from the path.

She walks over to you and Popplio.

"Howdy," she says introducing herself. "That bubble caught my eye! You see, I could really use some help from a Water type. I run a farm not too far from here. Well, if something doesn't happen soon, there won't be much farm to run…"

The farmer explains that it hasn't rained in some time and her land is experiencing a drought. There is no water for her crops. She's wondering if you and Popplio might be able to help her.

To follow the farmer back to her farm to see what you can do, go to **PAGE 10**.

Or, if you want to stay focused on the journey you've just begun, you can tell the farmer about a lake you saw on your walk. To point her in the direction of the lake, continue reading.

"Hm, I guess you are the one who is truly in need of guidance," the farmer says revealing her true identity—the Kahuna of Akala Island.

"Olivia!" you say with surprise. "I didn't realize it was you."

Suddenly, a lump forms in your throat. Taking on an Island Challenge with Kahuna Olivia would have been the most direct way to earn the Z-Ring and Z-Crystal you need to make a Z-Move. Normally, you would have jumped at the chance to ask her for the opportunity, but now it seems impossible. It's clear Olivia doesn't feel you're ready for an Island Challenge.

"I know you're new to Alola. Why don't I show you around?" Olivia offers.

"That would be awesome!" you reply, hoping to get to know her and the island better.

To follow Olivia, continue reading.

Olivia leads you through an area so lush, you have to push giant tree leaves out of your way with each step. You are moving as quickly as you can and you're glad you returned Popplio to its Poké Ball. You can barely keep up with the Kahuna. This is one steep climb!

But you suddenly realize you're at a rock wall. Where did she go? You look up.

"Give me your hand," Olivia says with hers outstretched.

She pulls you up to the rock ledge and you sit down next to her. The view of Akala Island is incredible. To the left is a farm with rows of red, pink, yellow, and orange flowers. "If you listen closely you can hear the rapids," Olivia says.

Wiiisssssssshhhh.

"I can hear it!" you reply. "Akala Island is an amazing place!"

Olivia smiles, "That it is. But it will only remain this spectacular if we all take care of it."

Kahuna Olivia explains that there is nothing more important to her than people and Pokémon of the Island living in harmony with nature. It's a delicate balance, one that must constantly be monitored.

"At the end of the Grand Trial, I might gift Trainers Z-Crystals, but that's not what it's all about," Olivia adds. "The goal of the Island Challenge is to help teach the next generation of Alolans to protect this special place. And I know, deep down inside, that caring nature is within you."

"It is!" you promise.

With that, Olivia bids you good luck on your journey with Popplio. She suggests you try another path and really explore Alola.

"I hope to see again, real soon," she says with a smile.

Olivia disappears into the forest. But before you leave the ledge, you need to share this unbelievable view with your Pokémon pal, Popplio. You take out its Poké Ball.

"Popplio!" it says with delight while taking in the view.

"Isn't it amazing?" you say. "I can't wait to travel around it all together!"

"Pop pop!" it agrees.

THE END

The farmer leads you through the Akala Island forest to her land. On the way, she tells you she started this farm not long ago hoping to help feed the local people and Pokémon.

"I thought the first harvest was hard," she says shaking her head, "But nothing has been as tough as this drought. Maybe my luck is turning around since I ran into a Water-type Pokémon. I'm so grateful for your help!"

"Popplio and I will do our best," you promise.

"Pop pop!" it nods.

A few more steps and you arrive at her farm. Row after row, the plants are sad and sagging, just as she had said. They need water—and fast!

"Hmmm," you mumble, thinking about how you can solve this problem.

To get to the root of the problem, proceed to **PAGE 11**.

Or, you could have Popplio water the plants using Hydro Pump. To have Popplio start the water works, go to **PAGE 15**.

She shows you around her farm. The reservoir is empty because there hasn't been a good rain in a while.

"Even in the dry season, it's never been this low," she says.

Next, you see the sprinklers used to spray water on the field. You ask Popplio to sniff it.

"Pop," it says shaking its head.

"There isn't a drop of water in there," you confirm.

There's only one more place to look. There's a pipe that runs deep underground and taps the water from the water table.

"The pipe goes down about a hundred feet," the farmer says. "It is attached to a pump on that tractor over there. Follow me."

The tractor's motor makes a loud sound, but you hear something else. You turn off the pump to listen closer and hear a faint cry.

"Diiiiiiiglett," it whimpers.

You examine the pipe with your flashlight and spot a sprig of blonde hair. An Alolan Diglett must be stuck in the line.

"Poor Diglett," the farmer worries. "We have to get it out of there!"

Not to mention, there is hopefully a lot of water behind that Diglett. You need to hatch a plan.

To hear the farmer's idea first, go to **PAGE 12**.
Or, to come up with your plan first, go to **PAGE 13**.

ALOLAN DIGLETT: Mole Pokémon

HEIGHT	0'08"
WEIGHT	2.2 LBS
TYPE	GROUND-STEEL

"I have an idea!" the farmer tells you. "I'll call on my Pokémon pals, Alolan Dugtrio. They've been so helpful digging around here for the crops, I bet they can get Diglett out."

She tosses her Poké Ball and the three-headed, blonde-haired Dugtrio arrives. The farmer explains the mission to them.

"Duuuugtrio!" its heads say in unison, ready to help.

Together they burrow into the ground through the pipe wall to set Diglett free. They clear a path and lead the way for Diglett to follow them back safely above ground... well, as much above ground as Diglett likes to be.

Diglett pops its head above ground and declares, "Diglett!"

Dugtrio is happy it could help. The farmer thanks you, too.

"We're always happy to help!" you say. "Right, Popplio?"

"Pop pop!" it agrees.

You and the farmer hope your paths cross again. But, for now, you're excited to get back to your training on the beach. After all, you have a Z-Move to practice!

THE END

ALOLAN DUGTRIO:
Mole Pokémon

HEIGHT	2'04"
WEIGHT	146.8 LBS
TYPE	GROUND-STEEL

"I have an idea to rescue Diglett and conserve water," you proclaim. "But I've never tried it before."

"I'm all ears!" the farmer replies.

"Well, Popplio and I have been training hard to use Hydro Vortex," you say showing her the Waterium Z Z-Crystal on the Z-Ring on your wrist. "Popplio and I should be able to use Hydro Vortex to direct the water in the pipe to fill the reservoir and restore your water supply."

She replies, "That's an awesome plan!"

This is your first time making your Z-Move! You would have liked more time to practice, but Diglett needs your help now.

"Popplio!" it says, ready to go.

"Diglett-lett-lett," you echo down the pipe, "We are here to rescue you-ou-ou."

Although Diglett is covered in mud, you can grab Diglett and pull it out with all of your might. You can feel the water rising up the pipe, so you tell the farmer and Popplio to get ready.

"Diglett!" it cheers back on the ground.

"Popplio, there's no time to waste!" you say while watching the water flood out of the pipe.

You cross your arms over your chest. Your Z-Crystal glistens with a light that radiates from the power within. You and Popplio wave your arms together. Your bond is creating the strength to make this Z-Move.

"Use Hydro Vortex!" you ask Popplio.

Popplio dives into the pipe, turning the flow into a twirling tower of water that rises above the farm. Your first Z-Move guides the water like a hose and pours into the reservoir.

"Thank you," the farmer says. "You two are amazing!"

Before you can reply, Popplio is covered in a ball of bright light. When the light fades, Brionne stands before you. Popplio evolved!

"Wow!" you say in awe of your Pokémon pal.

"Briiiiii!" it replies giving you a hug.

"I'd love to have you over for a proper thank you," the farmer says. "But I have to start tending to my plants before the sun sets."

So, you say goodbye to the farmer and Diglett and hit the road back to the beach. You can't wait to see what more Alola has in store for you and Brionne!

THE END

BRIONNE: Pop Star Pokémon

HEIGHT	2'00"
WEIGHT	38.6 LBS
TYPE	WATER

"Okay, Popplio, use Hydro Pump!"
you ask.

Popplio snaps into action. It starts
twirling like a sprinkler as it shoots a
stream of water onto the fields.

"Awesome!" the farmer says. "Thank you for the help. That watering should hold us for another day or so."

"It was our pleasure," you reply.

"Pop poplio!" it agrees.

You say goodbye to the farmer and head down the path to the beach to practice your Z-Move. You can't wait to get the chance to use it in a battle soon! So, it's time to get back to training.

THE END

"Okay, let's go!" you say to Popplio.

"Pop!" it agrees.

You begin to run towards the path to catch up with the wild forest Pokémon pack of Gumshoos and Yungoos. They're moving so fast, they're kicking up a cloud of dust.

Just as you think you're getting close, there is a fork in the road. At the center is giant tree with a trunk so high it looks like an umbrella casting a big circle of shade. It has long vines that almost touch the ground. It is so large it divides the path into two. Did the Pokémon pack go left or right? You can't tell.

To go left, continue reading. To go right, try **PAGE 24**.

You finally catch up with the pack of Gumshoos and Yungoos at a local lake. It seems these wild Pokémon are in an athletic club working out together.

"Gumshoos gumshoos gumshoos!" the leader counts as they all stretch in unison.

"Gumshoos!" it commands, ordering them to line up.

But Gumshoos isn't the only one shouting. Suddenly Crabrawler appears.

"Craaaaaaabrawler!" Crabrawler yells trying to shoo the Gumshoos away from the pool.

"Guuuuuuum!" it snarls back.

It looks as if they're about to battle, so you decide it's time to step in.

If you think Crabrawler is upset because the pool is too small, you can try to make it bigger with a Z-Move and go to **PAGE 18**.

Or to battle Crabrawler, go to **PAGE 24**.

YUNGOOS:
Loitering Pokémon

HEIGHT	1'04"
WEIGHT	13.2 LBS
TYPE	NORMAL

GUMSHOOS:
Stakeout Pokémon

HEIGHT	2'04"
WEIGHT	31.3 LBS
TYPE	NORMAL

CRABRAWLER:
Boxing Pokémon

HEIGHT	2'00"
WEIGHT	15.4 LBS
TYPE	FIGHTING

"Popplio and I are here to help!" you say.

All the Pokémon are looking at you, wondering what you're going to do. You look at the shiny Z-Ring and Waterium Z Z-Crystal on your wrist. You think this is the perfect time to use them because there are Pokémon in need!

"Let's do it, Popplio! Just like we practiced," you command.

You cross your arms over your chest and the Z-Crystal glows so brightly it covers the area. You and Popplio begin to dance in sync.

You can feel the power of the Z-Move ready to make a splash!

"Now Popplio, use Hydro Vortex!" you cheer.

The Hydro Vortex swings around the lake, making the pool of water much bigger.

"It's working, Popplio!" you cheer.

The lake may be bigger, but now the water is shallow. The low level of water reveals one angry inhabitant.

"Grrrrrrr!" a giant Gyarados shouts at the Pokémon on shore.

"Uh-oh," you mutter.

So that's why Crabrawler was trying to stop the Yungoos and Gumshoos from getting in the pool! You must restore the peace and it won't be easy with a growling Gyarados.

To battle Gyarados, turn to **PAGE 19**. To have Popplio fill up the lake using Hydro Pump to appease Gyarados, go to **PAGE 20**.

GYARADOS:
Atrocious Pokémon

HEIGHT	21"04"
WEIGHT	518.1 LBS
TYPE	WATER-FLYING

"Okay, Popplio, you ready?" you ask your pal.

"Pooooplio!" it nods.

Gyarados is a Water- and Flying-type Pokémon, so Popplio's Water-type attacks won't do much. If you could distract Gyarados, you could help Gumshoos and Yungoos make a run for it.

"Popplio, try Water Gun!" you say with your fingers crossed.

"Poppliiiiiooooooooooooo!" it says, firing a stream of Water Gun at Gyarados' head while Gumshoos and Yungoos flee.

Popplio's Water Gun has made Gyarados woozy. It's swaying back and forth like it's close to being knocked out. Something's not right.

"Crab crab!" Crabrawler says, scurrying to help Gyarados.

"Popplio, stop!" you shout. "I think Gyarados needs Nurse Joy."

Using the Xtransceiver on your wrist, you call the local Pokémon Center and tell Nurse Joy about Gyarados.

"I'll be right there!" Nurse Joy vows.

Continue onto **PAGE 22**.

"Popplio, use Hydro Pump!" you ask. "Aim it down at the edge of the lake, so it doesn't hit anyone."

"Pop pop Popplio!" it says, turning on Hydro Pump like a hose.

"Gyyyyyrrrrr," the giant Gyarados says with a smile, swimming in the bigger lake.

"Phew!" you whisper, relieved that Gyarados is happy.

When the lake is full, Crabrawler motions for all the Pokémon to jump in.

"Yungoooos!" the first Yungoos says diving in.

Soon, the rest of the team follows. Crabrawler and Popplio decide to go for a swim, too. You smile, happy to have made a big splash as a newcomer to Alola.

THE END

"Okay, Popplio, use Bubble Beam!" you say, starting the battle with Crabrawler.

"Poppp poppp poppp!" Popplio says, firing a spray of bubbles.

Crabrawler dives into the lake to dodge the attack. Popplio jumps in after it, but gets caught in Crabrawler's claws.

"Popplio!" you cry as you race to the edge of the lake.

You see Crabrawler is showing Popplio some Pokémon eggs at the bottom of the lake. Crabrawler was trying to warn you and protect them. You must find a way to get the Pokémon to swim somewhere else.

"Yungoos, Gumshoos, I have an important message," you begin. "There are fragile Pokémon Eggs at the bottom of this lake. It's too shallow to go swimming here. Why don't we all head to the beach instead? I know the way!"

The Yungoos and Gumshoos look at each other and nod.

"Right this way," you say, pointing the team down the path.

Before you get out of earshot, you turn around and say, "Thank you, Crabrawler!"

And with that, you, Popplio, Yungoos, and Gumshoos are on your merry way. Together with your new Pokémon friends, you have plenty of fun in the sun at the beach.

THE END

"Gyyyyyrrrados," it sighs, laying down in the lake with its head resting on the shore.

"I'm so sorry Gyarados. I never meant to hurt you or your home," you say. "I promise help is on the way."

"Popliooo," it adds.

Just then, Nurse Joy and Blissey arrive and snap into action. They examine Gyarados. Nurse Joy has Blissey get a special medicine out of her bag. Gyarados drinks it and sighs.

"It's all my fault, I never should have tried to make the lake bigger," you apologize.

"I know you were only trying to help and you did the right thing by calling me," Nurse Joy says. "Here in Alola, nature is abundant but only if we nurture it."

"Nurse Joy, is Gyarados going to be okay?" you ask.

"After taking this medicine and a good rest, definitely!" she says. "But I think filling more water in its home lake would also help."

"Popplio, that sounds like a job for us!" you say.

"Pop pop!" it agrees.

You ask Popplio to use Water Gun again, but this time to aim it down into the lake. The attack now works like a hose and the water level begins to rise.

"That's it! Keep up the good work, Popplio" you rave.

"Crab Crabrawler!" it adds, cheering Popplio on.

Gyarados slips back into the water and swims around. It's feeling better! Suddenly, it jumps out of the water and scoops up Crabrawler and Popplio to come swim with it.

"Thank you, Nurse Joy and Blissey!" you say.

"Thank you for caring for the wild Pokémon. I think you're going to fit right in here in Alola," she says with a smile.

"Blissey!" it agrees.

"Crabrawler, you deserve a big thank you, too! I'm sorry I didn't understand that you were trying to help Gyarados. But just know, Popplio and I will always be there to help!" you promise.

"Crabrawler!" it says with a nod as it splashes around with its new pal Popplio.

THE END

BLISSEY: Happiness Pokémon

HEIGHT	4'11"
WEIGHT	103.2 LBS
TYPE	NORMAL

You finally catch up with the pack of Pokémon, but it's because they're trapped. In the path before them is a huge silver robot. Its feet are spikes. Its hands are claws. Its head is an electrified cage. Behind a glass visor where its heart should be, lurks this mecha's evil makers— Team Rocket.

"Not much of a chase when they all come runnin' to us!" Meowth squawks with delight at the sight of the Pokémon pack.

"I think we're going to need a bigger cage!" Jessie says with a smirk.

James pulls a lever. The cage opens.

"Oh no! Look out," you warn the wild Pokémon, but it's too late.

The robot bends down and snags a clawful of Yungoos and Gumshoos. They get tossed inside the cage.

You must act fast to help the Pokémon pack, but what should you do? You realize the path has lead you back by the ocean. You could use the Z-Move Hydro Vortex to wash up Team Rocket's plans. But you and Popplio have never used a Z-Move before and there isn't a moment to lose. Perhaps using a big Hydro Pump would work?

To have Popplio use Hydro Pump to send them blasting off, turn to **PAGE 26**.

Or, to use your first Z-Move head to **PAGE 27**.

MEOWTH: Scratch Cat Pokémon

HEIGHT	1'04"
WEIGHT	9.3 LBS
TYPE	NORMAL

"Okay, Popplio, now!" you shout.

"Poppppplioooooo!" it cries, hosing down Team Rocket's Mecha with Hydro Pump.

The robot sizzles under the sheet of water. The cage opens and the wild Yungoos and Pokémon are free again!

Suddenly, an electrical explosion emerges from the chest of the robot and sends Jessie, James, and Meowth into the sky.

You rush back to the robot to help put out the fire before it reaches the forest.

"Popplio, use Water Gun," you ask.

"Popppliooo!" it says, shooting a stream of water that ends the blaze.

You can't believe Popplio's Attacks are so strong! All that practice is paying off and you feel ready to try your first Z-Move. Perhaps your next adventure will be taking on the Island Challenge?

THE END

"Popplio, quick, to the ocean!" you shout.

You and Popplio race to the shore.

The Waterium Z Crystal shines from the Z-Ring on your wrist as you cross your arms at your chest. A blue glow bathes you both. But before Popplio can dive into the deep blue sea, you see that Team Rocket Robot is running away.

"Oh no! Popplio, let's go," you yell, racing over with your pal.

You need to try something else—and fast!
To have Popplio spray the Mecha with Water Gun, continue reading.

Or, if you want to rally the wild Yungoos and Gumshoos to help battle the robot, head to **PAGE 29**.

"Water Gun, now, Popplio!" you shout.

"Poppppppp!" it yelps, hitting the back of the robot with a sharp stream of water.

"Nice try, ya twerp!" Meowth laughs.

"We're not done trying. Again!" you ask Popplio.

"Popppppppppppppppppp!" it yelps, firing Water Gun with all its might.

Shhhhhhhhhhh. You can hear the electricity sizzle as it races through the robot. A great jolt runs through it.

Zap! Team Rocket is thrown into the sky.

"We're blasting off agaiiiiiiin!" Jessie, James, and Meowth whine in a chorus.

Thwap! The cage door opens.

You help Gumshoos and Yungoos exit one at a time to avoid the electric energy. They thank you for your help.

"Hooray, Popplio! You saved the day," you say.

You wish you had a chance to make your first Z-Move, but you know you'll get another chance. No matter what, you and your best pal Popplio are always happy to help Pokémon in need. After all, that's the Alola way!

THE END

"Gumshoos, Yungoos, Popplio, let's work together to stop Team Rocket! Follow me!" you instruct, leading the way.

Together you race through the forest. You follow the robot, but stay hidden by traveling through the nearby brush. Luckily, the bulky robot is slow and your team is quick on their feet. In no time, you have passed the robot.

"Perfect!" you say to yourself as you spot a tall tree up ahead.

You ask Yungoos and Gumshoos to dig around the roots. Next, you ask Popplio to wet the ground with Water Gun. They snap into action and soon the tree is wobbling.

"Awesome job!" you cheer.

You ask your Pokémon friends to step aside and help you push.

"Uhhhhh!" you yelp, pushing the tree over.

Timberrrrrrr! With a big thud, the tree lands across the dirt path.

"Oh no! We're on a collision course with a log!" James shouts.

"Which lever makes the robot stop?" Jessie yelps.

"I don't know, pull them all!" Meowth panics.

"They're getting away!" Jessie whimpers.

"We've got bigger problems," James points out as the robot loses its balance from the fleeing Yungoos and Gumshoos.

Team Rocket gets thrown from the teetering robot into the sky.

"We're blasting off again!" they shout.

And not a moment too soon, as the robot crashes face down on the path.

"Hooray!" you cheer. "Thanks for your help!"

Team Rocket scrambles to stop the robot from hitting the log and it works! But Meowth accidentally pulls the lever that opens the cage. Gumshoos and Yungoos make a break for it, sliding down the shiny robot like it was a slide.

As you say good-bye to Yungoos and Gumshoos, you're left with one thought. You really have learned to appreciate the importance of nature in Alola.

How lucky there was such a big tree growing right on this spot! It's clear you need to plant a new tree to replace the one used to stop Team Rocket.

"Popplio!" it agrees.

You and your pal Popplio set out on a new adventure to find the perfect seed to plant.

You can't wait to see your pal Litten. You unzip your backpack and choose its Poké Ball.

"Litten, I choose you!" you cheer, tossing the Poké Ball into the air.

"Rrrrawrrrr" it purrs as you pet it hello.

You and Litten have really worked hard training. You've taken every battle challenge for practice. And now you're ready to make your first Z-Move!

There's just one hitch—you need a Z-Crystal!

Z-Crystals can be found on mountains and Alola has plenty of them! In fact, you see one peak to the north with lots of nubs and ledges. To travel to that mountain, continue reading.

You and Litten take a dirt path that leads to the mountain. But as you get close, you hear a ruckus. Something fishy is going on at the bottom of the mountain.

You signal for Litten to follow you into the forest. You carefully step over all the plants and flowers.

Thwap! Oof! You were so careful about watching the ground, you walked right into a tree branch.

"Hey, what was that?!" you hear someone ask.

"Probably just a wild Pokémon," someone replies.

"Let's catch it!" he says.

"What did I tell you? We have to focus on the mission!" someone shouts.

You breathe a sigh of relief. But you are curious. What is this mission? You motion to Litten to follow you and hide behind a shrub to get a closer look.

Through the leaves, you can see three thugs wearing black and white—it's nasty Team Skull! They're after a Z-Crystal on the mountainside.

You only have one option: fight. To battle them, continue reading.

Luckily, Team Skull hasn't spotted you yet. Your loyal pal Litten is looking at you for direction. You know you'll have to make the first move.

You can see the three Team Skull members clearly. Pink-haired Rapp and long-haired Zipp are following the orders of their blue-haired leader, Tupp. Rapp is standing on Zipp's shoulders trying to reach the Z-Crystal.

What you need now is a strategy. How are you going to strike?

If you'd like Litten to use Flamethrower to heat the Z-Crystal so it's too hot to touch, continue reading.

Or, to use Flame Charge to scare Team Skull away with a battle, proceed to **PAGE 35**.

You need to work fast, but you think it will be best if you stay hidden. Litten is ready to fire.

So you whisper your instructions, "Shoot Flamethrower right at the Z-Crystal!"

Litten aims a fierce flame stream straight at the precious Z-Crystal.

"Whooaaaa-ooaaa-oooaaa!" Rapp responds as she nearly slips off Zipp's shoulders, shocked by the fiery attack.

"Who's that?" Tupp shouts at the woods. "You're gonna get it!"

"Don't worry, Tupp," Rapp says, reaching as far as she can. "I got—ouchie ow ow!"

As soon as Rapp gets her hands on the flaming hot Z-Crystal, she has to immediately drop the scorching stone.

"Nooooooo!" Zipp yells, while watching the Z-Crystal fall.

Continue reading.

"I'll distract Team Skull. Go grab that Z-Crystal," you tell Litten.

You pop out of the bushes. "Are you the great, famous, amazing Tupp?!" you say, pretending to be a fan.

"That's me," Tupp says, turning to face you with a smirk.

"Then you must be Rapp and Zipp of the awesome Team Skull," you add.

While they're distracted, Litten pounces on the Z-Crystal and holds it in its mouth. Faster than you can say Breakneck Blitz, it scampers back into the woods.

"Salandit, get out here!" Tupp orders, throwing three Poké Balls.

"Okay, Litten, it's time to try our first Z-Move!" you suggest.

Litten places the Z-Crystal in your hand. You snap the red diamond Firium Z into the Z-Ring around your wrist. You and Litten begin to move in sync, getting ready to strike.

Litten blasts Team Skull back in a massive Inferno Overdrive ball of fire. Kapow! Team Skull and Salandit are unable to battle.

"Our first Z-Move!" you say, hugging your Pokémon pal.

Litten purrs with pride. With your special friendship and amazing Z-Move, you're ready for more fun in Alola!

THE END

SALANDIT: Toxic Lizard Pokémon

HEIGHT	2'00"
WEIGHT	10.6 LBS
TYPE	POISON-FIRE

"Litten, use Flame Charge!" you ask.

"Huh?!" Rapp turns, surprised to see Litten. "Look out!"

Covered in a fiery orange glow, Litten chases Team Skull. Tupp responds quickly to stop it in its tracks.

"Salandit, use Flame Burst now!" Tupp orders, tossing three Poké Balls.

A comet of fire soars from Salandit towards Litten. The Fire Cat Pokémon is fast and dodges the attack. Salandit might be able to protect the nasty trio of Team Skull, but they can't stop Litten!

What's your next move?
If you want Litten to try Fury Swipes, go to **PAGE 37**.

To use Flame Charge again, head to **PAGE 36**.

You think of a smart strategy and put it into action.

"Litten, use Flame Charge," you ask.

Litten, inside a fireball, races toward the three Salandit and topples them like bowling pins. While it's up close to the Toxic Lizard Pokémon, you throw a curve ball.

"Now Litten, Fury Swipes!" you say, surprising your foes.

Litten claws the Salandit trio.

"Rrrrrawrrrrrrrr!" it growls.

The Toxic Lizard Pokémon run into the woods, scared of brave Litten.

"Hey! Get back here!" Tupp yells while chasing after them.

"You did it, Litten!" you cheer.

Now that the Z-Crystal can't fall into the wrong hands, you're ready to earn it. You find the perfect place to climb.

"There it is!" you say, within reach of the Firium Z.

You steady your footing and release one hand to grab the glowing red Z-Crystal. "I got it!" you celebrate.

"I can't wait to make our first Z-Move!" you tell Litten. "Let's look for more adventures in Alola!"

THE END

"Litten, use Fury Swipes!" you ask.

Litten bravely approaches the three Salandit and tries to claw them all, but it's sorely outnumbered. The trio surrounds Litten.

"Rrrrrawr," Litten growls while standing its ground.

"Nice try, but you messed with the wrong guys," Tupp remarks. "Salandit, use Venoshock!"

The poison slime oozes from Salandit and covers Litten. It is left unable to battle.

"Ha! Told ya," Tupp mocks.

You rush over to Litten and hold it in your arms.

"I got you, Litten," you say, returning it to its Poké Ball.

You can't let Team Skull get that Z-Crystal. And now, without Litten, nothing stands in their way. So you think fast and use your Xtransceiver to call Officer Jenny and alert her to the thugs.

"I'm nearby. I'll be right over," she promises.

The minute you hang up, you hear sirens.

"She really is c-c-c-close!" Zipp blubbers.

"We better get out of here!" Rapp whines.

Team Skull runs away into the forest. Seconds later, Officer Jenny pulls up in her truck.

"Officer Jenny, thank you for coming!" you say. "Just the sound of your sirens scared them away from stealing the Z-Crystal."

"I'm glad to hear it!" she replies. "I'd like to thank you and Litten for your help. I'll stay in the area just in case."

She takes off in her truck to patrol the forest. The Z-Crystal sparkles from the mountainside. It is there for the taking, but you can't think about Z-Crystals when Litten needs you!

You race your Pokémon pal over to the nearest Pokémon Center. You're sure Nurse Joy will help Litten and you will be back in action soon. But nothing is more important than the wellbeing of your buddy.

THE END

"Rowlet, I choose you!" you cheer while tossing your Poké Ball.

"Rrrrr!" your Pokémon pal coos, happy to see you.

Rowlet is your best friend and that makes it the perfect partner to take on an Island Challenge. If you're successful, you will earn a Z-Crystal from Olivia, the Kahuna of Akala Island.

To see if Rowlet can spot the Olivia's location from the sky, continue reading. Or, to hike to the local Pokémon Center, turn to **PAGE 56**.

Rowlet soars up into the sky. It circles around the area looking to spot Olivia. It sees many people and Pokémon in Alola. In the fields, it sees Bounsweet and Alolan Rattata. Near a lake it spots Crabrawler. Over by the mountain, it sees Rockruff and Lycanroc. Up in the trees, it spots Pikipek and a woman wearing a yellow jacket—could that be Olivia?! Rowlet swoops down to get a closer look. It is! But that's not all it sees.

Rowlet quickly flies back to guide you to Olivia. You race through the brush as fast as possible, barely able to keep up with Rowlet. Although you're out of breath and your legs feel tired, you keep going. If Rowlet is flying this fast, there must be trouble.

Proceed to **PAGE 41**.

BOUNSWEET:
Fruit Pokémon

HEIGHT	1'00"
WEIGHT	7.1 LBS
TYPE	GRASS

PIKIPEK:
Wood Pecker Pokémon

HEIGHT	1'00"
WEIGHT	2.6 LBS
TYPE	NORMAL-FLYING

ALOLAN RATTATA:
Mouse Pokémon

HEIGHT	1'00"
WEIGHT	8.4 LBS
TYPE	DARK-NORMAL

ROCKRUFF:
Puppy Pokémon

HEIGHT	1'08"
WEIGHT	20.3 LBS
TYPE	ROCK

When you finally reach Olivia, you see why Rowlet was so upset. She's standing next to a cage with a crying Ledian.

"Poor Ledian fell into a Poacher's trap," Olivia tells you.

Who can think about asking for an Island Challenge when there is a greedy Poacher trying to steal Ledian?! You realize the only challenge that matters right now is freeing this poor Pokémon.

"Don't worry, Ledian. Rowlet and I are here to help," you vow.

To have Rowlet use Peck to break the lock, go to **PAGE 42**.
Or, to ask Kahuna Olivia to help you find Totem Lurantis and ask for its help, turn to **PAGE 43**.

LEDIAN: Five Star Pokémon

HEIGHT	4'07"
WEIGHT	78.5 LBS
TYPE	BUG-FLYING

"Okay Rowlet, use Peck to pop that lock!" you ask.

Using its beak, Rowlet strikes the lock with a powerful prod of Peck. Zzzzzap! The second its beak touches the cage, its whole body buzzes with electricity.

"Oh no, Rowlet!" you cry.

You race to save Rowlet and get shocked, too. The poacher rigged the cage! Ledian was not harmed but Rowlet needs some care from Nurse Joy. You return it to its Poké Ball to rest.

"I'm so sorry that we weren't able to help, Ledian," you say.

"You two did your best!" Olivia says, thanking you. "I'll stay here with Ledian and Officer Jenny is on her way. We'll make sure Ledian is free again in no time!"

You say goodbye and head for the local Pokémon Center.

"When you are both feeling better, I'd be happy to accept an Island Challenge from you!" Olivia says.

Perhaps you won't get the chance today, but you hope it will be someday soon.

THE END

"Kahuna Olivia, do you know where Totem Lurantis lives?" you ask.

"Of course, it is just down this path. Let me show you the way," she replies.

Kahuna Olivia quickly leads you to a big cave nearby. Sunshine peaks through a break in the rock roof. This is the cave that Totem Lurantis calls home.

You know that Totem Lurantis will help you, if you earn its respect. To do that, you must challenge it to a battle. You waste no time and step right up.

"Totem Lurantis, I am here to challenge you to a battle!" you declare into the cave.

"I, Kahuna Olivia, have brought this challenger to you Totem Lurantis. Please grant this brave Trainer a battle," Olivia adds.

Suddenly, its Ally Pokémon, Castform appears. Its face is bright orange and it has a halo of lighter orange balls that make it look like the sun. It must be Sunny Form.

"Castform!" it says, accepting your challenge.

To ask Rowlet to start with Razor Leaf, go to **PAGE 44**.
To have it use Brave Bird, proceed to **PAGE 46**.

CASTFORM: Weather Pokémon

HEIGHT	1'00"
WEIGHT	1.8 LBS
TYPE	NORMAL

"Rowlet, use Razor Leaf!" you instruct.

"Rrrrr rrr rrrr rrrr!" Rowlet squawks, firing a round of sharp leaves at Castform.

But Castform is too quick and dodges your attack. Castform harnesses the sunshine and covers the cave battlefield with Sunny Day. Next, it adds a fierce blast of Flamethrower.

"Rrrrrr!" Rowlet moans, struggling to hang on.

"Castform!" it chants, shooting another fiery stream of Flamethrower.

With the added power of Sunny Day, Castform's Flamethrower is unstoppable. Rowlet is left unable to battle.

"Rowlet, I'm so proud of your bravery," you tell your pal. "Now you deserve a good rest at the Pokémon Center."

You return Rowlet to its Poké Ball and walk over to Olivia to apologize.

"I was really hoping we could help you and Ledian," you tell her.

"I know. I sure could have used the help of an awesome Trainer like you," she says while patting you on the back. "But don't worry, I'm not going to let anything happen to Ledian!"

You begin to walk out of the cave to find the local Pokémon Center when you hear a loud noise. Thwap!

It looks like a wild Alolan Sandslash passed by and saw that Ledian was trapped. It used a cutting Metal Claw to break the cage lock. Ledian kicks open the door to the cage and climbs out to freedom!

"Nice work," Kahuna Olivia says.

"Hooray!" you celebrate.

You and Olivia are so relieved Ledian is free! But you have Rowlet to care for now, so you return to the Pokémon Center.

"Wait, one more thing," Kahuna Olivia calls after you. "When you and Rowlet are ready, I'd be honored to accept an Island Challenge from a brave team like you two!"

"Well, then I guess you'll be seeing us again real soon," you say with a smile.

THE END

ALOLAN SANDSLASH:
Mouse Pokémon

HEIGHT	3'11"
WEIGHT	121.3 LBS
TYPE	ICE-STEEL

"Rowlet, are ya ready?" you ask.

"Rrrrrr!" it replies.

"All right! Start with Brave Bird," you instruct.

Rowlet swoops in, covered in a bright white light. It lands a direct hit with a Brave Bird.

"Cassssssstform!" it yelps, responding with a Flamethrower burst.

"Dodge it!" you shout. "Then use Brave Bird again!"

Rowlet soars back into the air to avoid the fiery Flamethrower. It then flies over Castform's head and swoops back around for a sneak attack of Brave Bird. Bam!

With that aerial tackle, Castform is knocked out. But the battle is really just about to begin.

"Now you will get the chance to battle Totem Lurantis," Olivia reminds you.

"Lurantis!" it announces its arrival.

You look up and see Lurantis standing on a rock ledge. It is so tall and noble. This is going to be quite a fight! You decide to make the first move and hope to use the element of surprise.

"Rowlet, can you start with Brave Bird again?" you ask.

"Rrrrrrr!" it responds, flying into action.

Bam! Rowlet lands a direct hit. Lurantis stumbles for its footing. It loses its balance and falls off the rock ledge and down before you. Kahuna Olivia gasps.

Suddenly, you have a sinking feeling in your stomach. What just happened? Maybe Lurantis is hurt? Maybe you were too excited and started the battle too soon? Maybe you accidentally did something mean? Or maybe you just won? Maybe Totem Lurantis won't want to keep battling now that you've started with such a strong move? All the maybes run through your head. But what are you going to do?

To see if Totem Lurantis is okay, go to **PAGE 48**. Or, to ask Totem Lurantis to help you get Ledian out of the cage, go to **PAGE 49**.

LURANTIS: Bloom Sickle Pokémon

HEIGHT	2'11"
WEIGHT	40.8 LBS
TYPE	GRASS

You and Rowlet race to Lurantis' side to see if you can help it up.

"Lurantis, are you okay?!" you ask.

"Luuuurantis," it says, opening its eyes.

"Would you like some help? Would you like me to get Nurse Jenny?" you ask.

Lurantis stands up. Luckily, it was surprised, but not hurt. Phew! You are so relieved.

Trainers are supposed to care for their Pokémon pals, but it takes someone with a lot of heart to care for all Pokémon. In return, Lurantis gifts you a Z-Crystal, Grassium Z.

"Wow, my first Z-Crystal!" you cheer. "I can't thank you enough! But I have one more favor to ask…"

You explain that Ledian is trapped in a cage. You are hoping Lurantis can use its fire beams to cut through the bars and set it free.

"Lurantis!" it responds, ready to snap into action.

Proceed to **PAGE 50**.

Totem Lurantis is happy to help a Pokémon in need. When you arrive at the cage, you see Ledian is very scared.

"Don't worry," you tell Ledian. "Lurantis is going to get you out of there."

"Lurantis!" it promises.

Totem Lurantis slices through three metal bars with the bright light beam it fires from its petal-like arms. Thwack!

Ledian rushes out of the cage. It hugs your leg. Then it hugs Olivia and Lurantis, too. It walks back into the forest but, before it disappears, it waves goodbye.

"Thank you for your help, Lurantis" Olivia says.

"You were awesome!" you agree.

"Lurantis," it says goodbye and returns to the cave.

Now it's time to ask Olivia for a chance at the Grand Trial!

"It's been a long day, come back another time. I'll remember you," Olivia says with a smile.

You and Rowlet go back down the path looking for more adventure in Alola. You know you'll return to Akala some day. And when you do, you'll find Kahuna Olivia and take her up on an Island Challenge.

THE END

Olivia leads you, Rowlet, and Lurantis back to the cage. Ledian is so happy to see you! And even happier to know Lurantis is going to set it free.

"Luuuurrrurantis!" it shouts, slicing through the bars of the cage. Whap! Whap!

Three bars fall to the ground. Ledian leaps out of the cage.

"Thank you, Lurantis! That was amazing," you say.

"Rrrr rrrrr!" Rowlet agrees.

"You deserve a big thank you too," Olivia adds.

"I'm always happy to help a Pokémon in need!" you reply.

Olivia looks into your eyes and says, "There are so many natural wonders in Alola from the environment to the Pokémon. I am not the only one who is here to protect them. In fact, there are many brave Trainers like you who help preserve this incredible place."

"I want to be one of those Trainers!" you respond. "I want to try the Island Challenge."

Olivia laughs and says, "Oh, so you know about that. Good! I accept your challenge."

The next step is the Grand Trial—a battle with her. Continue reading.

Deep in the forest of Akala, a stone monument appears. The entrance is triangle-shaped and painted with splashes of bright magenta.

There are columns covered in faded red, yellow, and green geometric shapes.

"This must be the place," you think, "The Ruins Of Life."

You and Rowlet take the stone steps down to a clearing. In the center is a big battlefield tiled in stone. White drawings are in each corner of the rectangular board. Colorful wildflowers surround this sacred spot.

Olivia enters. She is ready to begin the Grand Trial!

"I'm glad to see you," she begins. "Now let's begin our island challenge—The Akala Grand Trial! I ask Wela Volcano, which nurtures Akala Island, and Tapu Lele, the guardian of all our island life, to watch over us during this challenge and give us strength."

And with that, the stage for the battle is set. But who will make the first move?

To call on Rowlet to start, go to **PAGE 54**.
To let Olivia begin, continue reading.

"Lycanroc!" Olivia says summoning her pal.

This Lycanroc is Midday Form with a big, bushy white tail. Now that Olivia has chosen her Pokémon, you are even happier to have your pal Rowlet with you.

A Flying- and Grass-type, Rowlet can take to the sky and has a helpful type advantage. But you notice another Pokémon friend is there, too. Peaking out from behind a bush to watch the battle is none other than Ledian.

It must have followed you. You smile, happy to see it again. But before you can say hello, Olivia has begun.

"Use Accelrock," Olivia says, kicking things off.

"Rrrrroc!" Lycanroc growls.

Covered in a white glow, Lycanroc charges at Rowlet. Rowlet dodges it by soaring straight up into the sky.

"Quick, use Rock Slide," Olivia adds.

Boulders swirl around Lycanroc, then fly straight for Rowlet. It maneuvers in the air to avoid them.

"Way to go, Rowlet! Now fire Razor Leaf!" you say.

Rowlet fires a group of beaming, green leaf blades at Lycanroc. The Wolf Pokémon dodges them with a jump. This is a tough battle between two fierce Pokémon. Olivia decides to use a Z-Move. She crosses her arms over her chest and is soon covered in a fiery glow. A burst of beams shoots from her to wrap Lycanroc and give it the fierce strength.

"Go Continental Crush!" Olivia instructs.

"Arrrrrooooo!" Lycanroc yelps, while leaping into the air above Rowlet.

Giant rocks rise up and roll into one massive round mountain. It is so big that it casts a complete shadow over the battlefield. Rowlet tries to fly out and dodge it, but it gets caught under the boulder. After that awesome Z-Move, it is left unable to battle.

"You are a great Trainer," Olivia tells you. "I am grateful for your help with the caged Ledian. I am glad we got the chance to battle."

You thank your pal Rowlet as you return it to its Poké Ball. Before you take it to rest at the Pokémon Center, Olivia suggests you try to catch another Pokémon pal—Ledian.

"Beeeeeee beee!" it smiles, running out before you.

You know having playful Ledian come along on your journey would be a blast! You take out a Poké Ball. Ledian nods to show you it is ready. With a single toss, Ledian disappears into the Poké Ball. As it flashes, you cross your fingers that it will work. Bing! That sound can only mean one thing—you have caught Ledian.

"Congratulations!" Olivia says. "Now I want you to train hard together and then come back and challenge me to another Grand Trial!"

"You have a deal!" you say, shaking Olivia's hand.

As you head to the Pokémon Center, you think about all of the adventures Alola has in store and how much more fun they are with good friends.

THE END

LYCANROC:
Wolf Pokémon

HEIGHT	2'07"
WEIGHT	55.1 LBS
TYPE	ROCK

"Probopass!" Olivia says, choosing her Rock- and Steel-type Pokémon pal.

Your battle strategy is to strike first and use the element of surprise. Before Probopass can get its first move in, you ask Rowlet to use Razor Leaf.

"Rrrrrrrrr!" it shouts, while shooting a sharp Razor Leaf.

Probopass gets hit, but shakes off the stream of leaves.

"Let's go, Zap Cannon," Olivia says.

"Stay put," you tell Rowlet.

Probopass prepares a dark ball of energy with yellow, electric tentacles. Just as it goes to fire, you tell Rowlet to soar straight up and dodge it.

"Awesome, Rowlet!" you shout to it up in the sky. "Now use Brave Bird!"

Rowlet speedily swoops back down and slams into Probopass.

"Proooo," it cries, falling over.

The Compass Pokémon gets back up. It's ready to keep battling!

"Probopass, use Magnet Bomb," Olivia says.

Probopass' three mini-noses fly off and begin to chase Rowlet through the air. Rowlet can't escape them. It's time to try your first Z-Move!

"Now, Rowlet!" you say, calling it back to the battlefield.

On your Z-Ring, the Grassium Z that Lurantis gifted you shines in the sunlight. As you clasp your hands at your chest, you are covered in a green glow that transfers onto Rowlet.

"Rowlet, use Bloom Doom!" you shout with excitement.

Rowlet bursts green light into a dome. The dome grows into a giant bright ball that bursts with an incredible explosion! Probopass is left unable to battle.

Olivia kneels next to her pal to thank it for the battle and returns Probopass to its Poké Ball.

"Congratulations," Olivia says. "It is my great pleasure to present you with another Z-Crystal, Rockium Z!"

"Thank you, Olivia, for accepting my Island Challenge" you say. "It was an honor to battle you."

With that, you and Rowlet bid goodbye to the Kahuna of Akala Island.

THE END

PROBOPASS:
Compass Pokémon

HEIGHT	4'07"
WEIGHT	749.6 LBS
TYPE	ROCK-STEEL

After a long trek through the forest, you are finally getting close to the Akala Pokémon Center. Your legs are tired, your feet hurt, but you're a Pokémon Trainer. Nothing will stop you from achieving your goals!

Then, suddenly, you hear a rustling noise coming from the forest. Brusssssh.

You ignore it and keep walking. But then you hear it again, louder this time. BRRRRUSSSSSSH!

What could it be? Maybe it's the wind? Maybe it's nothing? Maybe it's something? Maybe you should stop and check it out?

To investigate what could be causing the noise, go to **PAGE 58**.
To stay on the path to the Pokémon Center, continue on to **PAGE 57**.

You spot a big wood building with an orange roof. An archway above the door has a Poké Ball drawn in red.

"This must be the Pokémon Center!" you say excitedly.

You walk through the front door. Inside there are Trainers patiently waiting to pick up their Pokémon, posters and pamphlets about Akala, and, of course, Nurse Joy with her aids Blissey and Comfey.

"Hello there, how can I help?" Nurse Joy greets you.

"Hi, Nurse Joy, I'm looking for the Kahuna of Akala, Olivia. Do you know where she is? I'm hoping to give the Island Challenge a shot!" you say proudly.

"That's a great ambition!" Nurse Joy replies. "But I'm sorry to say that Kahuna Olivia is traveling at the moment. She went to Melemele Island to see Professor Kikui. I'm not sure when she'll be back."

You contain your disappointment and thank Nurse Joy. You and Rowlet will have to return another day. In the meantime, there is plenty to explore on Akala Island. So you leave the Pokémon Center to see what fun you can find.

THE END

COMFEY:
Posy Picker Pokémon

HEIGHT	0'04"
WEIGHT	0.7 LBS
TYPE	FAIRY

"Rowlet, I need your help!" you
say, tossing its Poké Ball. "Can you
see someone or something from the
sky? I heard a strange noise coming from the forest."

"Rrrrrrr!" Rowlet says, snapping into action.

Rowlet soars into the air and circles the area.

"Rrrrr rrrrr rrrr!" it signals you.

"Where is it, Rowlet?" you ask.

It flies down to lead you off the path through the trees and over
rocks to the exact spot. Before you is an injured Oricorio. It is
yellow and lanky with poofs of feathers on its wing tips and
ankles—it must be Pom-Pom Style. The Dancing Pokémon is
wrapped in a thorny vine. It must have gotten caught while
practicing its fierce dance moves.

"Oooorrrricorrrio," it cries out.

It is flailing its wings to try to escape its vine shackles, but it's just
getting wrapped up even more.

"Oricorio, Rowlet and I are here to help you," you promise.
"Stay still and I will unravel the vines."

Oricorio flaps its wings as you move towards it. It is a little nervous.

"Rrrrrr," Rowlet adds, reassuring it.

Oricorio nods and remains still. You carefully unwind the vines. You notice that poor Oricorio has marks on it from being pricked by the thorns. It takes time, but you're able to finally set it free.

"Orrrrrri Orrricorrrrio!" it sings, thanking you for its liberty.

You tell Oricorio that it now needs to rest. You know Nurse Joy could take care of its wounds from the thorns.

"Rowlet and I can take you to see her," you say. "It's not very far. I can carry you."

Oricorio's nature is to want to dance, but it knows its first move should be to the Pokémon Center. Continue reading.

ORICORIO:
Pom-Pom Style

HEIGHT	2'00"
WEIGHT	7.5 LBS
TYPE	ELECTRIC-FLYING

You walk into the Pokémon center, holding Oricorio in your arms. Blissey and Nurse Joy rush over to you with a bed. You lay Oricorio down and tell Nurse Joy that it got caught up in some thorny vines while dancing.

"I have just the thing to heal these cuts," Nurse Joy says.

"Orrrrrricorrrio," it thanks her.

Later that evening, Nurse Joy says, "Oricorio is healing just fine. I'm hoping it will feel ready to dance tomorrow."

"That would be great!" you reply.

The next day Oricorio is feeling fine.

You, Rowlet, and Oricorio exit the Pokémon Center.

"I guess this is goodbye," you say to Oricorio.

You part ways. But as you walk away, it calls out. You stop and turn around. Oricorio is running to catch up.

"Orrrrri!" it calls after you.

To have Rowlet use Peck to start the battle, continue reading. Or, to let Oricorio make the first move, go to **PAGE 62**.

Rowlet begins the battle with Peck. Its beak beams with a white light as it races towards Oricorio. The Dancing Pokémon dodges it with a graceful leap.

Oricorio begins to sway, shaking its Pom-Poms in the air to start Revelation Dance. A bolt of electricity bursts from its fluffy feathers and sends Rowlet up into the sky. Zap!

The Grass Quill Pokémon falls to the ground.

"Rowlet!" you cry out with concern.

"Rrrrrr," it says woozy, but still ready to battle.

Oricorio starts to sway again. You're worried Rowlet will take another direct hit of Revelation Dance.

"Orrrrriiiiiiiiii!" Oricorio yelps while letting out a beam of bright, electrified light from its Pom-Poms.

The bolt strikes Rowlet, but something is different this time. An amazing, sparkling glow surrounds the Grass Quill Pokémon. When it fades, a new, evolved form appears—Dartrix! It proudly squawks to declare its arrival.

"Wow, Dartrix!" you welcome it with awe.

Dartrix powers up a ray of light. It must be creating a powerful Solar Beam. Oricorio responds by swaying from left to right to stop it with Teeter Dance.

"Don't look at Oricorio or it'll put you in a trance with its dance," you warn Dartrix.

Luckily, Dartrix quickly breaks out with a Solar Beam so strong it knocks out Oricorio. Flash!

You act fast and toss your Poké Ball. You and Dartrix watch it blink.

Bing! You just caught Oricorio!

"Dartrix, you were awesome!" you say, thanking your pal. "You might have a new form, but you'll always be my old friend."

Between Oricorio and Dartrix, you have so much to look forward to while exploring Alola. You can't wait to get back on the road and find the Kahuna of Akala, Olivia—and that's just what you do. You're hoping she'll take you up on an Island Challenge. But who knows what fun adventure will await you next? You'll have to keep going to find out.

THE END

Oricorio waves its wings in the air and begins to dance.

"Rrrrrr!" Rowlet replies, ready to battle.

Oricorio rubs its Pom-Poms together and tries to muster a zap of electricity. It rubs its Pom-Poms again and throws all of its energy into raising its wings to create a bolt. Fizz.

Its electricity is on the fritz. Oricorio looses its footing and falls to the floor.

"Oricorio!" you cry, rushing to its side.

You carry your friend back to Nurse Joy at the Pokémon Center and tell her what happened.

While Oricorio rests, Nurse Joy calls Kahuna Olivia. She tells her all about how kind you've been to Oricorio. She then summons you over to her screen to meet the Kahuna of Akala Island.

"You are just the kind of Trainer we need here in Alola!" Olivia tells you. "When you're ready, I'm hoping you'll come find me to try the Island Challenge!"

"It would be a dream come true to battle you!" you tell Olivia.

"Well, then I expect you, Oricorio, and Rowlet to train hard. You know, sometimes, my Grand Trial is a double battle," she replies.

You decide to wait for your friend, Oricorio. Continue reading.

The next day, Oricorio is feeling better.

"Orrrriiii Orrriii!" it sings, showing you and Nurse Joy its dance.

It begins to rub its Pom-Poms together and they pulse with electricity.

"Oh no! There's no firing inside the Pokémon Center, Oricorio!" Nurse Joy says. "You can spark your Pom-Poms outside. Congratulations, I think you're ready to be discharged!"

"Hooray!" you cheer for your friend.

As you leave the Pokémon Center together, Oricorio has one thing on its mind—a rematch!

"Let's do it!" you reply, ready to battle.

"Rrrrrrr!" Rowlet agrees.

Oricorio starts the battle by using Revelation Dance. With its Pom-Poms swaying above its head, Oricorio does a few special steps. Then it fires a bright bolt at Rowlet.

The Grass Quill Pokémon quickly swoops up into the sky to dodge it, then shoots back a Razor Leaf swirl. While Oricorio is caught in the storm of leaves, you tell Rowlet to soar down and strike with Brave Bird. Bam!

"Rowlet, race towards Oricorio with Tackle!" you shout.

But Oricorio quickly changes plan and surprises you with Mirror Move. It mimics Rowlet and grabs its foot.

"Orrrri!" it shouts, stopping Rowlet mid-step.

Oricorio tries to smack Rowlet with Double Slap, but Rowlet escapes its grip and blows back green blades with Razor Leaf.

"Awesome, Rowlet! Use Tackle, again," you ask.

Rowlet knocks Oricorio over with Tackle. So while the Dancing Pokémon is off its feet, you toss a Poké Ball.

Oricorio disappears into it and it begins to flash. You hope you caught your friend, but only time will tell. The Poké Ball stops flashing and beeps. Bing!

"Yay!" you celebrate. "I couldn't have done it without you, Rowlet."

With your old pal Rowlet and your new buddy Oricorio by your side, you can't wait to continue on your journey and perhaps even seek a double battle challenge.

THE END